This book belongs to:

......................................................................

This edition published by Parragon Books Ltd
in 2017 and distributed by

Parragon Inc.
440 Park Avenue South, 13th Floor
New York, NY 10016
www.parragon.com

Written by Margaret Wise Brown
Illustrated by Olivia Chin Mueller
Edited by Suzi Heal
Designed by Lauren Tiley
Production by Juliet Fountain

ISBN 978-1-4748-4657-8

Printed in China

# Walk with Me

## PaRragon

Bath • New York • Cologne • Melbourne • Delhi
Hong Kong • Shenzhen • Singapore

Will you come for
a walk with me?

Into the woods, where the willow tree
washes its leaves in a shiny pool,
Where the sun is warm
and the shade is cool.

Will you come?
Will you come for a walk with me?

Down to the brook, where I'm sure we'll see ...

...Turtles and lizards and fishes and frogs,
And dragonflies and pollywogs.

Will you come?
Will you come for a walk with me?

Into the woods, where the bumblebee
Buzzes and hums in the wild thorn tree.

Will you come?
Will you come for a swim with me?

Down where the fishes swim in the sea,

Far from the hum of a bumblebee.

Will you fly?
Will you fly through the air with me?

Up where the birds fly dreamily,
Soaring through clouds
on a wild blown spree.

O, come fly through the air with me!

But if you should feel too sleepy
to come for a walk with me,

Out into the world stretching endlessly ...

We could still dream
how it would be,
If you came for a
walk with me.